Whatever.

Level 9 – Gold

Helpful Hints for Reading at Home

The focus phonemes (units of sound) used throughout this series are in line with the order in which your child is taught at school. This offers a consistent approach to learning whether reading at home or in the classroom.

HERE ARE SOME COMMON WORDS THAT YOUR CHILD MIGHT FIND TRICKY:

water	where	would	know	thought	through	couldn't
laughed	eyes	once	we're	school	can't	our

TOP TIPS FOR HELPING YOUR CHILD TO READ:

- Encourage your child to read aloud as well as silently to themselves.
- Allow your child time to absorb the text and make comments.
- Ask simple questions about the text to assess understanding.
- Encourage your child to clarify the meaning of new vocabulary.

This book focuses on developing independence, fluency and comprehension. It is a gold level 9 book band.

Whatever.

Written by
William Anthony

Illustrated by
Drue Rintoul

Chapter One

From Top to Bottom

"Phil, please. We need you to take this job," begged Whittaker. "You're the only person left. Everyone else has turned it down."

Phil puffed out his chest. "I said I DON'T WANT IT!" he replied. He added some extra oomph to his words that time.

Whittaker was right. Phil really did speak like he was leadership material.

Of course, that was exactly what Phil didn't want to be.

Phil and Whittaker both lived in the whimsical village of Bottom. Many of the people who lived in Bottom demanded a lot from whoever was their leader.

There were rumours that this was why Stephanie took a break from being leader. There were other rumours that Stephanie had taken more than a break. There were even rumours that Stephanie had taken more than a break all the way to the Philippines on the other side of the planet.

Nobody knew exactly what had happened to Stephanie, but Bottom was in need of a new leader. All Phil knew was that he wasn't going to be it. He was an old man who yelled at clouds and needed naps after each meal.

Whittaker didn't know what else to do. She had asked Crazy Steve, Odd Nancy, Tattoo Stan, Tattoo Stan's nephew, Joseph the Wise (and his mum) and now Phil. They had all refused.
"There is one person you haven't asked," huffed Phil.
"There is?" replied Whittaker. "Who?"

Chapter Two

The Last Hope

There was a loud knock at the door. Nina didn't notice it. Anything happening away from her tablet screen wasn't important. Whittaker phoned Nina's butler, Murphy. He gave Nina a swift tap on the shoulder.

"What?" she barked at Murphy.
"What a horrid attitude," said Murphy. "There are some people outside who would like to talk to you."
"Whatever," grunted Nina. Murphy was used to that word.

Nina was a difficult child. She was a seven-year-old grumble box. That's what Murphy called her, anyway. Whenever anybody asked her anything, she would snort back the word 'whatever'.

Most of the time, it made life a real whirlwind for Murphy, but Murphy was not a fool. Sometimes he would trick her.

"Your mother called. She said Grandma was in trouble for pole vaulting over elephants again," he would say, to test if she was paying attention.
"Whatever," Nina would reply.
Then he would get sneaky.
"Can I take the afternoon off work?" he would slip in.
"Whatever!" Nina would grunt. Before she'd realised what she had said, Murphy would be gone.

Today wasn't the time for tricks, though. Bottom needed a hero. A nervous Whittaker stood at the foot of Nina's bed.
"I need to ask you a question, Nina," whimpered Whittaker. "Will you be the new leader of Bottom?"
There was a long pause...
"Whatever," Nina mumbled.

"R-r-really?" stammered Whittaker. She didn't think it would be that easy. "Are you sure?"
"I SAID WHATEVER!" shouted Nina.
Murphy was sat with his head in his hands.
He knew things were about to get ugly.

Chapter Three

Funkytown

The next day, The Bottom Telegraph's headline read: 'Finding Nina: The search for a new leader is OVER'. The people of Bottom felt like they could relax again. Murphy didn't.
"Be careful, Nina. The people of Bottom are very demanding," Murphy warned her.

"Whatever," she said.

There was a knock at the door. It was Tattoo Stan. He had a question for Nina.

"Nina, now that you're the leader, do you think it would be alright for me to keep a pet dolphin?" he asked.

Murphy started to make his point. "See Nina, this is exactly what I mea-"
"Whatever," sighed Nina. She was too busy playing Puffin Party on her tablet to care.
"Whoopee!" cried Stan. He skipped down the path, whistling a merry tune. Murphy slammed the door.

"Really, Nina? A pet dolphin? Why don't you let someone keep a gorilla too, or maybe even a white tiger?" ranted Murphy. "You need to take care with your decisions or Bottom will end up in a whole lot of trouble!"

There was another knock at the door.
A long, winding line of people were waiting.
One by one, they asked Nina for something.
Nina only had one way of answering questions, which meant a lot of new rules were made that afternoon.

Joseph the Wise asked Nina to make a rule that people had to greet each other by doing a handstand. "Whatever," said Nina.
Odd Nancy wanted telephones to be banned.
She wanted to replace them with megaphones.
"Whatever," said Nina.

Nina even let Crazy Steve keep a gorilla and Tattoo Stan's nephew keep a white tiger.

Joseph's mum was not as wise as him. She got Nina to make a rule that only dogs could use steering wheels in cars. Dog drivers were odd, even for Nina.

Whittaker even got Nina to rename Bottom. Now it was called Funkytown.

Every time Nina said 'whatever', Funkytown got crazier.
Murphy pulled Nina to one side. "Nina, I warned you about these people! They are nuts! When will you learn?" he whispered.

Nina didn't listen. For every person in the line, a new rule was made.

The streets of Funkytown were very funky indeed. Half of the villagers were on their feet, while the other half were stood on their hands, thanks to Joseph's handstand rule. Other people were leaning out of their windows, shouting to each other with megaphones, thanks to Odd Nancy's rule. Gorillas and white tigers were walking on the pavements, while poodles and pugs were driving on the roads.

'Whatever' was the most dangerous phrase of all in Funkytown.

Chapter Four

Nice One, Phil

Funkytown's new rules had gone down well.
It even turned out that dogs were rather good
at driving. They had started a taxi company
called K9 Cabs, where people paid in biscuits.

For one person, though, Funkytown wasn't
quite funky enough. Phil hobbled his way up to
Nina's house.

"Having you as our leader has been a triumph!" he said.

"Whatever," replied Nina.

"But there are so many rules. The old folk like me can't keep up," he chuckled.

"I think we should just have one rule," said Phil, as a sinister smile grew on his face. "That one rule should be... that there are no rules!"

Murphy had heard enough.

"Nina, wait!" he yelled. "You cannot make this rule. You'll destroy this village!"

Murphy pleaded with Nina. "If you make this rule, then I will leave. I won't watch my beautiful Bottom be turned into a lawless Funkytown," he blubbered.

"So, what's your decision? Can we make the rule?" asked Phil.

"Whatever," grunted Nina.
Murphy's heart sank. He grabbed his coat and walked off into the rain.

Phil, on the other hand, jumped to his feet. He ripped off his suit. Underneath, he had a vest, leather trousers and more tattoos than Stan. He put on a helmet.

"Just to let you know, Nina, having no rules means that you're no longer the leader of Funkytown," Phil sniggered. He jumped on his motorcycle and pulled a wheelie as he drove off into the chaos. Nina finally said a new word.

"Whoops."

Chapter Five

Give Me My Bottom Back!

One month later, Funkytown was a mess. K9 Cabs was now run by the gorilla and the white tiger, people worshipped saxophones and the only food left was whipped cream. In the middle of the madness, Nina was handing out pamphlets.

Nina had spent a month in the mayhem she had made. It helped her understand why she should have cared about the choices she made as leader. Now, she was ready to turn Funkytown around, but she needed the help of an old friend.

MURPHY

Nina's plan was coming together. She decided to make a speech to the people of Funkytown. Murphy shuffled in at the back of the crowd.

"Whatever," said Nina. Murphy sighed, but Nina carried on. "This village can be WHATEVER we want. It can be a huge Funkytown mess, or it can be the beautiful Bottom it used to be. I have five new rules I think we should follow, here for all to see. I say we clean this place up and bring back our Bottom! Who's with me?"
The crowd cheered. Murphy smiled at Nina and she smiled back.

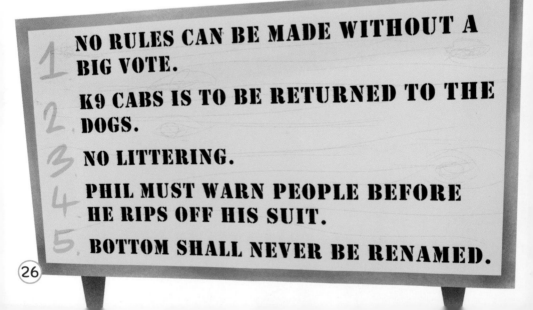

1. NO RULES CAN BE MADE WITHOUT A BIG VOTE.
2. K9 CABS IS TO BE RETURNED TO THE DOGS.
3. NO LITTERING.
4. PHIL MUST WARN PEOPLE BEFORE HE RIPS OFF HIS SUIT.
5. BOTTOM SHALL NEVER BE RENAMED.

It took some time, but the village of Bottom was finally back to normal. Murphy forgave Nina after she had learned her lesson, but she still had a trick up her sleeve.

"I have something to confess," Nina told Murphy. "I made a sixth rule..."

Nina opened the door to her bedroom. The gorilla was playing a saxophone, the dolphin was reading The Bottom Telegraph and the white tiger was napping on the bed.

"These guys don't have to leave. Can we keep them?" asked Nina.

"Whatever," giggled Murphy.

Whatever.

1. What did Phil like to yell at?

2. What did Murphy call Nina?

   a) A grumble box

   b) A grumpy chair

   c) A mean box

3. What pet did Tattoo Stan want to keep?

4. Why did Murphy walk off into the rain?

5. How do you think Nina felt when she realised what she had done to Bottom? Do you think you would be a better leader? What would you do differently?

©This edition published 2021.
First published in 2020.
BookLife Publishing Ltd.
King's Lynn, Norfolk PE30 4LS

ISBN 978-1-83927-014-7

Whatever.
Written by William Anthony
Illustrated by Drue Rintoul

An Introduction to BookLife Readers...

Our Readers have been specifically created in line with the London Institute of Education's approach to book banding and are phonetically decodable and ordered to support each phase of the Letters and Sounds document.

Each book has been created to provide the best possible reading and learning experience. Our aim is to share our love of books with children, providing both emerging readers and prolific page-turners with beautiful books that are guaranteed to provoke interest and learning, regardless of ability.

BOOK BAND GRADED using the Institute of Education's approach to levelling.

PHONETICALLY DECODABLE supporting each phase of Letters and Sounds.

EXERCISES AND QUESTIONS to offer reinforcement and to ascertain comprehension.

BEAUTIFULLY ILLUSTRATED to inspire and provoke engagement, providing a variety of styles for the reader to enjoy whilst reading through the series.

AUTHOR INSIGHT:
WILLIAM ANTHONY

Despite his young age, William Anthony's involvement with children's education is quite extensive. He has written over 60 titles with BookLife Publishing so far, across a wide range of subjects. William graduated from Cardiff University with a 1st Class BA (Hons) in Journalism, Media and Culture, creating an app and a TV series, among other things, during his time there.

William Anthony has also produced work for the Prince's Trust, a charity created by HRH The Prince of Wales that helps young people with their professional future. He has created animated videos for a children's education company that works closely with the charity.

This book focuses on developing independence, fluency and comprehension. It is a gold level 9 book band.